COMING

GOD BLESS QUEEN VICTORIA!

STEWART ROSS

COMING ALIVE

GOD BLESS QUEEN VICTORIA!

STEWART ROSS

Illustrated by
SUE SHIELDS

EVANS BROTHERS LIMITED

TO THE READER

God Bless Queen Victoria! is a story. It is based on history. The main events in the book really happened. But some of the details, such as what people said, are made up. I hope this makes the story easier to read. I also hope that ***God Bless Queen Victoria!*** will get you interested in real history. When you have finished, perhaps you will want to find out more about Queen Victoria and the time when she lived.

Stewart Ross

This book is dedicated to the pupils and staff of the 1999 Summer Literacy School, Castle Community School, Deal

Published by Evans Brothers Limited
2A Portman Mansions, Chiltern Street
London W1M 1LE

© copyright in the text Stewart Ross 2000
© copyright in the illustrations Sue Shields 2000
First published 2000

All Rights Reserved. No part of this publication may be reproduced, stored in a retrieval system or transmitted in any form, or by any means, electronic, mechanical, photocopying, recording or otherwise, without prior permission of Evans Brothers Limited.

British Library Cataloguing in Publication Data
Ross, Stewart
God Bless Queen Victoria! – (Coming Alive)
1. Victoria, Queen of Great Britain – Juvenile literature
2. Great Britain – History – Victoria, 1837-1901 – Juvenile literature
I. Title
941'.081

Printed in Spain by Gráficas Reunidas, S.A.

ISBN 0 237 520311

Contents

THE STORY SO FAR page 7
1 **'MY HORRID DUTY':**
   Victoria refuses to change the ladies of her court. She gets into serious trouble. **page 11**
2 **THE QUESTION OF MARRIAGE:**
   The young queen thinks about marriage and remembers Prince Albert. **page 17**
3 **'A THOUSAND TIMES YES!':**
   Prince Albert comes to stay. Victoria asks him to marry her. **page 23**
4 **A ROYAL WEDDING:**
   Victoria and Albert are married. The British people are suspicious of Albert. **page 29**
5 **ALBERT'S DREAM:**
   The royal family grows. Albert tells Victoria his latest idea. **page 35**
6 **THE GREAT EXHIBITION:**
   Albert plans a festival of work and peace, and finds a building to put it in. **page 41**
7 **'SPARROW HAWKS, MA'AM':**
   Victoria visits the Crystal Palace. The Duke of Wellington solves a problem. **page 47**
8 **'GOD BLESS QUEEN VICTORIA!':**
   Huge crowds come to see Queen Victoria open the Great Exhibition. **page 53**

THE HISTORY FILE
What Happened Next? **page 57**
How Do We Know? **page 59**
New Words **page 61**
Time Line **page 62**

THE STORY SO FAR...

THE KINGS FROM HANOVER
In 1714 the people of Britain had to make a choice. They could either have Roman Catholic monarchs of the Stuart family, or Protestant monarchs from the Hanover family. They chose the Hanoverians, who were German. The first Hanoverian, George I, couldn't even speak English, and he felt much more at home in Hanover than Britain. But the next four Hanoverian kings, George II, George III, George IV and William IV were all much more British than German. Even so, Britain kept up close links with Germany.

PRINCESS VICTORIA
The Hanoverians were an unlucky family. George III went mad. George IV and his brother William IV were not respected, and during their reigns the monarch was not taken very seriously. To make matters worse, neither George nor William left an heir. After William's death the crown was due to pass to Princess Victoria. Victoria was the daughter of William's brother, the Duke of Kent. His German wife, the Duchess of Kent, was not

very bright. The Duke died the year after Victoria was born, leaving the girl in the hands of her foolish mother. However, knowing that she would be queen one day, Victoria was determined to behave and set a good example to her people.

QUEEN

Victoria became queen at the age of 18. This was an enormous responsibility for such a young girl, especially as her silly mother was not much help. In those days women had little to do with politics, and Victoria had no father or husband to advise her. Instead, she relied on the kindly prime minister, Lord Melbourne. She was also helped by the shrunken and elderly Doctor Stockmar, a German friend of her Uncle Leopold. Another German, Baroness Lehzen, was also close to the queen. She had once been Victoria's governess and now she stayed on at court as a friend. The queen nicknamed her 'Daisy'. But when Victoria felt really fed up, she went into her room and chatted with her spaniel, Dash.

Portrait Gallery

Queen Victoria

Prince Albert

Sir Robert Peel    **Duke of Wellington**    **Joseph Paxton**    **Lord Melbourne**

Duchess of Kent    **Princess Victoria**    **Prince Albert**    **Prince Ernest**

Baroness Lehzen   **Committee Member**

9

C.B.E.C.

JERVOIS PRIMARY
SCHOOL

CHAPTER ONE

'MY HORRID DUTY'

Victoria sat bolt upright in her favourite chair in the Blue Chamber. Before her, looking rather old and sad, stood her dear friend Lord Melbourne. 'It can't be helped, Ma'am,' he said with a sigh. 'My government isn't wanted any more, and I must go.'

Queen Victoria   **Lord Melbourne**

'But you can't!' said Victoria fiercely. Melbourne raised an eyebrow. 'I mean, I don't want you to. You have been so kind and helpful to me.'

Melbourne smiled. 'There will be other ministers, Ma'am, and they will serve Your Majesty as well as I.'

11

Victoria jumped to her feet. 'Fiddlesticks!' she cried. 'Who will be like you, Lord Melbourne? Tell me that!'

Melbourne rubbed his hands together. 'Well, there's the Duke of Wellington.'

'Too old and too deaf,' snorted the queen. Actually, she liked the Duke but was not in the mood to say so.

Duke of Wellington

'Then there's Sir Robert Peel?'

'Cold and horrid,' Victoria snapped, her eyes filling with tears. 'Like yesterday's gravy.'

Melbourne explained once again to the queen that personal feelings did not come into it. If Sir Robert was Parliament's choice, then she had to accept him. It was her duty.

The moment he left, Victoria ran to her room and burst into tears. 'Bother my stupid duty!' she sobbed. 'Bother! Bother! Bother!'

Victoria had pulled herself together by the time Sir Robert arrived. But she couldn't stop herself shuddering when he came into the room. He walked awkwardly, pointing his toes like a dancing master. And his smile looked like the silver handle on a coffin.

'Good day, Ma'am,' he began, bowing his head.

'Is it?' Victoria asked rudely. Sir Robert gave one of his coffin handle grins, but said nothing. The queen then explained that it was her duty to ask him to become her prime minister.

Queen Victoria   **Sir Robert Peel**

Sir Robert nodded and replied calmly, 'I should be honoured, Ma'am.' He then talked about government business for a while. Victoria tried not to look bored. Finally, just when she thought he was about to leave, he said carefully, 'And, of course, if I am to be prime minister, Your Majesty must change some of the court ladies. We cannot have ladies of Lord Melbourne's party around you. The new ladies must be of my party.'

Victoria could hardly believe her ears. 'Change my ladies?' she cried. 'Never! They are my friends. Prime ministers run the government, not my household.'

Sir Robert looked very stern. 'May I remind Your Majesty of your duty?' he said carefully. 'The people must see you helping the prime minister. A new prime minister means new people at court, including your ladies.'

Victoria's eyes narrowed. 'I won't do it,' she said firmly.

After a long pause, Sir Robert said slowly, 'Very well, Ma'am, then I can't serve you as prime minister. You'll have to try Lord Melbourne again.' He bowed and left the room.

When Sir Robert had gone, Victoria rushed off to find Baroness Lehzen. 'Daisy!' she cried, running up to her old governess and giving her a huge hug, 'I've won! I won't have cold fish Peel as prime minister after all! I can have lovely Lord M back!'

The baroness looked startled. What on earth was Victoria talking about?

14

After the queen had explained, the baroness's face looked grim. 'If I may say so, Ma'am,' she said sternly, 'I think that was rather unwise.'

And so it turned out. The queen's behaviour caused a huge row and made her very unpopular with Sir Robert's friends and supporters.

Victoria was deeply upset at the news. 'Oh dear!' she whispered to Dash when they were alone. 'What have I done? It's so lonely being queen. Where can I find a real friend to help me with my horrid duty?'

Dash

Chapter Two

The Question of Marriage

Queen Victoria

Victoria did not enjoy the next few weeks. She read in the papers that all kinds of pompous and important people had criticised her for falling out with Sir Robert Peel. She didn't know her duty, they said, and she ought to be taught a lesson.

To make matters worse, when she was riding with her courtiers in Windsor Park, a complete stranger rode up and asked her to marry him. 'Your Majesty!' he cried, 'A handsome young lady like you shouldn't be living alone! It's not right. Be a good girl and take me as your husband. You won't find a better.'

Guards quickly took the man away, and later she heard that he was a well-known nuisance. Even so, his words set her thinking. Maybe she should marry. It would be so nice to have a kind, sensible husband to help her. Someone she could trust and share her problems with. But was there

17

such a man? At the back of her mind she knew there might be one, but he was miles away. Who knows when I'll see him again? she thought sadly.

Two days later the question of marriage came up again. This time it was Victoria's mother, the empty-headed Duchess of Kent, who mentioned it at lunch. Actually, she did more than mention it. She almost shouted it.

'Darling Victoria,' she began, waving to the butler to refill her wine glass, 'you need a man!'

'I beg your pardon, Mother?' said Victoria coolly. Sometimes she wished her mother would learn to keep her mouth shut.

Duchess of Kent   **Queen Victoria**

'Come along, darling,' continued the Duchess, 'you know, a man. A big, strong, hairy one, with whiskers. You can't be queen on your own. Queens always have kings.'

18

'Queen Elizabeth didn't,' interrupted Victoria.

'Eh? You and your learning! Books give you silly ideas. You'd be better off without them, like your mother. Anyway, Elizabeth was different. As I was saying, queens always have kings, just as kings always have queens. They go together like ... well, like love and marriage! Hee, hee!'

Victoria winced. She knew the sort of man people wanted her to marry. There was the revolting Prince George of Cambridge – even the dogs ran away from him. Then there was blind Prince George of Cumberland, and the oafish Prince Alexander of Orange. As for the peacock Duke of Brunswick, she would rather give up being queen than marry him. The way he looked at anything in skirts ... Ugh!

The Duchess was still prattling on. 'And so I hope you'll take my advice, Victoria darling, and get yourself married soon. There's nothing like a man about the palace, I promise you. And I do know what I'm talking about, after all.'

When her mother had gone, Victoria went into her favourite Blue Chamber to read. She picked up the latest instalment of Charles Dickens' *Nicholas Nickleby*. Dickens was all the rage and she loved his stories. Normally, she couldn't wait to read the next episode. But today ... well, today she just couldn't concentrate.

Her mind drifted back to 1836, the year before she became queen. During the spring her German cousins, the eighteen-year-old Ernest and his seventeen-year-old brother Albert, had paid her a visit. The princess had been much taken by the pair.

Ernest was tall and polite, but his nose was a bit awkward and his mouth a little flabby. But Albert was just beautiful. He was the same age as Victoria, tall and pale, with large blue eyes and lovely light brown hair. He was clever, too, and funny. The way he played with Dash had everyone in stitches.

Prince Ernest   **Prince Albert**

Victoria had often thought of Albert since then. He had written her the sweetest letter at the time of her coronation, and there had been talk of his returning to England. But it was now three years since they had met, and he had never come.

The queen set down the Dickens and stretched out a hand to tickle Dash's ear. 'You liked him, Dashy, didn't you?' she whispered. The dog looked up at her with large, sorrowful eyes. Victoria smiled. 'Yes, I know you did. And shall I tell you a secret? Don't tell anyone, Dashy, but I think he's the only man in the world I could ever really love.'

CHAPTER THREE

'A THOUSAND TIMES YES'

On 10 October 1839 Queen Victoria woke up with a headache. When she came down to breakfast, she was told that a madman had been arrested during the night for throwing stones at her windows. Oh dear! she thought, it's going to be one of those difficult days.

Later that morning she put on her outdoor clothes and went for a walk in Windsor Park. She had not gone far when she saw a messenger running towards her. Not more problems! she sighed, waiting under a dripping oak tree for the man to catch up with her.

Queen Victoria

'I beg your pardon, Ma'am,' he panted, 'but I have some important news.'

'Yes?' nodded Victoria. 'What's the disaster now?'

The messenger looked confused. 'Disaster, Ma'am? I don't think so. I have been asked to inform Your Majesty that the Princes Ernest and Albert of Saxe-Coburg have arrived in England and wish to stay at Windsor.'

23

The queen's heart jumped. 'Princes? At Windsor? When?'

'Tonight, Ma'am.'

Although the queen did her best to appear dignified, she couldn't help the blood rushing to her cheeks. 'Tonight?' she gasped. 'How sudden! Well, don't just stand there! Hurry back to the castle and tell them to get rooms ready. And food. And music. Yes, Prince Albert loves music. We must give him a wonderful welcome.'

Noticing a twinkle in the messenger's eye, she added, 'And Prince Ernest. We must give them both a wonderful reception. Now, off you go!'

Albert had grown. He looked pale and tired after a rough Channel crossing, but in Victoria's eyes he was more handsome than ever. To her delight, he seemed overjoyed to see her.

The next three days were a whirl of rides, concerts, banquets and dances. The young couple were always together, talking and laughing. They were a perfect match. Where Albert was reserved, Victoria was outgoing; where she was disorganised, he was tidy and careful. She had no father, and found in Albert a father-figure. He had no mother, and found in Victoria all the warmth and affection he had missed as a child.

...he was more handsome than ever.

After dinner on the third day the queen found herself sitting next to Lord Melbourne. 'Fine pair, those German cousins of yours, Ma'am,' he said.

Victoria smiled. 'Yes, My Lord. Very fine.'

Melbourne coughed. 'Prince Ernest seems very intelligent, Ma'am.'

'Maybe, My Lord, but I find Prince Albert far more intelligent,' Victoria replied quickly. She gave Melbourne a challenging look.

Queen Victoria   Lord Melbourne

'Ah!' Melbourne said slowly. 'I thought that's how it is, Ma'am.' Victoria lifted her fan to hide her blushes. 'Cupid's arrow is very sharp, Ma'am,' he went on. 'But may I humbly suggest you wait, perhaps a week, just to see how things turn out? For the sake of her people, a queen must make the right marriage, Ma'am.'

Victoria rose to her feet. 'So kind of you to advise me, My Lord,' she said politely, 'but I really must be going.' As she went off to find Albert, she said to herself, 'Seven days? Silly old Lord M! I can hardly wait seven hours!'

The next morning Prince Albert went to the library. He needed to look up one or two English words he had heard the servants whispering. But before he could find a dictionary, a footman came in and asked him to join the queen in the Blue Closet. The prince nodded, nervously smoothed down his hair and went off to find Victoria.

Prince Albert

Queen Victoria

The queen was wearing her favourite pink gown. When Albert came into the room, they stood staring into each other's eyes for a minute, saying nothing. Eventually, Victoria spoke. 'You know why I have asked you here, Albert, don't you?' He nodded. 'And because I am a queen and you are a prince, you know why I have to ask,

27

don't you?' Again he nodded. 'Then,' she continued, her voice almost in a whisper, 'my dear, dear Prince Albert of Saxe-Coburg, will you marry me?'

A huge grin spread across Albert's face. 'Yes, my beloved Victoria! Yes! A thousand, thousand times yes!'

CHAPTER FOUR
A ROYAL WEDDING

Queen Victoria

Victoria and Albert kept their engagement secret for a month. In private they exchanged rings, locks of hair and hundreds of kisses. But in public they pretended they were just cousins who got on well together.

It did not take people long to see through this act. The servants gossiped, and Albert was always seen at the queen's side. He even went with her to inspect the guard, and when he put his cape round her shoulders to keep out the cold, most people realised what was going on. So it was no great surprise when the queen officially announced her engagement.

Victoria was happier than she had ever been. Albert was her dream man: kind, wise, intelligent and good looking. With him to help her, she reckoned she could cope with anything. Even the icy Sir Robert Peel.

Prince Albert

29

She was even happier when the Duchess of Kent agreed that after the wedding she would set up a home of her own in Clarence House. 'Well darling,' she laughed, 'you won't be wanting an old thing like me around, not now you've found your man!' Victoria pretended to be sad that her mother was leaving, but in her heart she was relieved.

However, not everything went well. Some politicians wondered why their queen had chosen to marry a German. Was there no suitable young Englishman? Victoria was thinking only of herself, they grumbled, not her people. They said unkind things about Albert in parliament, too, and refused to let him be called "King Albert".

This upset Victoria deeply. But it could not spoil her wedding, which took place in the Royal Chapel on 10 February 1840. Dressed in military uniform, Albert was more handsome than ever. As for the bride, no one had ever seen Victoria looking lovelier. She wore a white satin dress and a diamond necklace that twinkled like stars on a frosty night. A wreath of orange blossom circled her brow.

The guests broke into a round of applause when the ceremony was over. Lord Melbourne, trussed up like a Christmas goose in a stiff new coat, nodded contentedly. Smiling broadly,

Victoria kissed her old Aunt Adelaide, the wife of King William. But when her mother came forward for a greeting, the queen only shook her hand. Not even on her wedding day could she bring herself to kiss the tiresome Duchess.

When they were alone together at Windsor Castle or Buckingham Palace, the life of the young couple was all joy and smiles. But the queen was still troubled by the way her people treated Albert. He was an outsider, and they did not trust him. They did not like a foreigner interfering in their affairs, and he was not allowed to be with the queen when she had official meetings with politicians.

One day, when the royal couple were talking privately with Lord Melbourne, the queen asked, 'My Lord, surely everyone can see that Prince Albert is the cleverest, hardest working man in the world? So why won't they let him be more useful?'

Queen Victoria　　　　**Lord Melbourne**

Melbourne looked the queen in the eye. 'The British are an island people, Ma'am,' he began. 'They are suspicious of all foreigners.'

'Well, they should grow up,' frowned Victoria. 'If their queen can love a foreigner, they should follow her example.'

Albert placed a hand on her arm. 'Of course, Ma'am,' he said gently. (He always called her "Ma'am" when other people were around.) 'But I pray you let His Lordship finish.' Victoria snorted but kept quiet.

Prince Albert

'Besides, if I may say so Ma'am,' Melbourne went on, 'some German members of your family have not lived perfect lives. Your uncle George IV, for example, was a little, er, wild at times. You took the prince to your heart in three days. It will take the British people three years, or more, to feel as you do. They will need time.'

'Ja, that is good,' said Albert eagerly. His English sometimes went to pieces when he was excited. 'Time is my friend. I will work and work

32

and work for my queen and her people. Then they will be seeing that their Prince Albert is a good German. And one day they will love him like their queen.'

Victoria smiled at Lord Melbourne. 'There you are, My Lord. Isn't he wonderful? My people will soon see that I married a hero. It is so obvious!'

CHAPTER FIVE

ALBERT'S DREAM

Victoria's first child was a girl. She was born in November 1840, almost exactly a year after Albert had arrived at Windsor. The delighted parents named her Victoria after her mother and grandmother, Adelaide after her aunt, Mary after Albert's mother, and Louisa because they liked the name. At home the little girl was known simply as 'Vicky'.

The next year Victoria had a baby boy. They named him Albert, of course, but also gave him the English name Edward, or 'Bertie'. Over the next ten years, came Alice, Alfred, Helena, Louise and Arthur. A host of nurses and governesses was hired to help Victoria look after the children. Even so, she had less time than before to spend on the things she found boring, such as politics. Luckily, Albert was always there to help.

Princess Victoria

Prince Albert

In time, as Lord Melbourne had predicted, the British people began to appreciate the hard-working Prince. He was interested in everything, from new drains to old paintings, and was always dashing about organising, advising and planning some improvement or other. No one minded, therefore, when he became Victoria's private secretary and stood at her side during her meetings with politicians.

Lord Melbourne

When Sir Robert Peel finally became prime minister, Albert got on well with him, too. Victoria soon came round to her husband's way of thinking.

Sir Robert Peel **Prince Albert**

'You're right again, my love!' she admitted. 'I suppose I was a bit hard on Sir Robert all those years ago. As you say, he is intelligent and good at getting things done.' Going up to her husband and giving him a kiss on the cheek, she added, 'But nowhere near as good as you, the wisest of all men!'

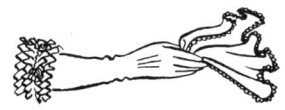

Both Victoria and Albert liked to travel. They visited different parts of the country, even calling on Sir Robert Peel in his country house, Drayton Manor. They also went abroad, travelling to Germany and France. Wherever they went, large crowds came out to greet them. Britain's little queen and her serious-looking husband won people's hearts almost everywhere they went.

One visit in particular stuck in Albert's mind. In 1843 he went with Victoria to stay at the Duke of Devonshire's grand mansion at Chatsworth. But it was not the house that Albert noticed so much as an enormous glasshouse in the grounds. It had been built by the Duke's head gardener, Joseph Paxton.

Joseph Paxton

'The man's a genius,' the Prince told his wife after he had spent a morning looking round it. 'It's amazing what you can do with glass and iron nowadays. Quite amazing.' Victoria nodded politely. She was not very interested in greenhouses, no matter how large they were. She left that sort of thing to her husband.

Albert might have liked glasshouses, but he did not like draughty palaces or castles. They were damp and unhealthy, he said, and the London smoke was bad for the children's health. Victoria agreed with him. So when Vicky was nearing her second birthday, the couple started taking long holidays in the country.

Their favourite places were Osborne, on the Isle of Wight, and the Scottish Highlands. On one of their Highland holidays they stayed at an old hunting lodge at Balmoral, deep in the remote glens. They immediately fell in love with the romantic hideaway, and came back each summer to escape the crowds and noise. To Victoria's delight, Albert arranged to buy the land and built a fairy-tale castle there.

One evening, during one of their stays at Balmoral, Albert first let Victoria into a secret. 'I have a dream, my love,' he explained, getting up and putting another log on the fire. 'We live in a

'The man's a genius.'

wonderful age. Railways. Workshops. Iron ships steaming all over the world. And peace, too. We have not had a war since the time of Napoleon. The Victorian Age is the finest in the history of mankind.'

The queen jumped. 'The what?' she asked.

'The Victorian Age. Named in honour of our wonderful queen. And I want to celebrate it with an enormous festival. It will be dedicated to work and peace. It will be like nothing ever seen before.'

'Oh Albert!' smiled Victoria happily, 'You are a wonder!'

Chapter six
The Great Exhibition

Victoria fully supported Albert's idea for a festival of peace and work. She would not hear a word said against it. When her old friend Baron Stockmar said he was alarmed by the cost, she told him not to be so boring.

She was more annoyed when Baroness Lehzen said the festival should be held in a railway station, because it was the only building big enough. 'Don't be such a numbskull, Daisy!' she cried. 'The Prince has all that under control.' In fact, the old governess's remark was not so silly. Albert himself did not yet know where the festival could be held.

Baroness Lehzen   **Queen Victoria**

Night after night he sat up into the small hours writing letters and making plans. In January 1850 he set up a committee to help him. They decided to call the festival the Great Exhibition. To encourage peace and co-operation between the nations of the world, they invited other countries to put on displays of their own, all under the same roof.

Although he was not keen on the smoke and dirt of London, Albert realised that the capital city was the only place to hold the Exhibition. The committee chose a site right in the middle - Hyde Park - and announced a competition for a suitable building.

Victoria followed the plans with great interest. But she was worried by how tired her husband looked. 'You look exhausted, Albert. You need a holiday,' she told him one morning. When he replied that he could not rest until the Great Exhibition was ready, the queen asked anxiously, 'Are you sure it's all worth it, dear?'

Queen Victoria

Prince Albert

'Worth it?' he gasped. 'My Angel, it's the most important thing I've ever done in my life.' When Victoria looked shocked, he added quickly, 'Apart from marrying you, my dear.'

The queen relaxed a little. 'Even so,' she went on, 'lots of people don't like the Exhibition idea. Parliament won't give it money. Smart ladies and gentlemen think it'll spoil the look of Hyde Park. Some businessmen believe the displays will give away their secrets. And I hear that the Tsar of Russia refuses to let his people come to London. He thinks they'll pick up dangerous ideas here, about freedom!'

Albert listened patiently until the queen had finished. 'I know not everyone approves,' he replied, 'but sometimes we have to take risks, don't we?'

'Maybe,' nodded the queen. 'It's strange, but when I was the wild one you were the careful one. Now we seem to have swapped places. So please take care, dear Albert. Please. It would be awful for both of us if the Exhibition was a disaster.'

The next day Albert and his committee went through the competition entries. There were 233 different ideas for an Exhibition building. One was a gigantic tent. Another was a sort of cathedral. Yet another showed a building that looked like Windsor Castle, made out of wood and canvas.

Albert went through them all very carefully. 'A fire risk,' he muttered over the Windsor Castle idea. The cathedral would take too long to build and be too expensive. The tent might blow away... . None of the designs were what he was really looking for.

'It's no good,' he sighed. 'They're all either too boring, too dangerous, too expensive, or too difficult. We'll have to hold another competition.'

'There is just one other entry, sir,' said a chubby man whose glasses were as thick as his thumbs. 'But it looked so ridiculous I was going to put it straight in the bin.'

'What is it?' Albert asked.

'Well, it's a sort of gigantic greenhouse.'

'A what? Let me have a look.'

Committee Member   Prince Albert

The man shuffled through his papers and pushed a scruffy set of drawings towards the Prince. 'Crazy, isn't it, sir?'

'They're all either too boring, too dangerous, too expensive, or too difficult.'

Albert glanced quickly through the sketches, then read the name at the top. 'Crazy?' he exclaimed. 'Why, sir, it's you who is crazy! This is the work of Joseph Paxton. I met him at Chatsworth. He's a genius.' He held the drawing up for everyone to see. 'This, gentlemen, is the building for the Great Exhibition.'

Joseph Paxton

CHAPTER SEVEN

'SPARROW HAWKS, MA'AM'

Victoria did not often see the Duke of Wellington nowadays. He was over eighty and deafer than ever. She was surprised, therefore, when one day he wrote asking to meet her. She agreed, and invited him to call at Buckingham Palace.

Duke of Wellington

After they had made polite conversation for a while, the queen asked the Duke why he wanted to see her. 'Eh?' he grunted, lifting a hand to his ear. 'Don't hear too well, Ma'am. Would Your Majesty mind repeating the question?'

'Why - are - you - here?' said Victoria carefully.

The Duke nodded. 'Thank you, Ma'am. I've come about the greenhouse.'

It was Victoria's turn to be confused. 'The greenhouse, My Lord? What greenhouse?'

Queen Victoria

'The thing in the Park. Don't

47

mind the Exhibition, Ma'am. Think it's a grand idea. But I don't like the damned greenhouse.'

Victoria frowned. She did not approve of swearing. 'Beg pardon, Ma'am,' apologised the Duke, 'but I just don't think it's any good.'

'Why not?'

'It'll get smashed by hailstones. And the sound of guns firing a salute. Too flimsy, all that glass.'

'Mr Paxton and the Prince have thought of everything,' Victoria replied firmly. 'The glass won't break. Besides, My Lord, how do you know it's flimsy? Have you seen it?'

'Beg pardon, Ma'am?'

Just as I thought, Victoria said to herself. 'Have you seen Mr Paxton's glasshouse, My Lord?' she asked again. 'The building they call the Crystal Palace?'

The Duke looked confused. 'No, Ma'am. Can't say as I have.'

'Then I will show it to you, My Lord. We will meet there next Tuesday, at 11 o'clock. Don't be late.'

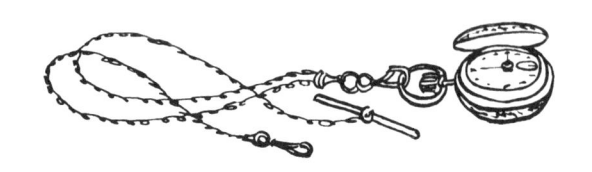

The Crystal Palace was indeed a wonderful structure. Gleaming and glistening in the morning sunlight, it rose above the Park like an enormous diamond. It was so tall that it completely covered several of the Park's ancient elm trees, which were left growing inside. And the sparrows that lived in their branches twittered merrily around the glassy galleries.

Victoria and her three eldest children arrived at exactly 11 o'clock. Vicky, Bertie and Alice, in smart new coats, were thrilled at being allowed to see their papa's wonderful Crystal Palace.

Princess Victoria (Vicky)   **Prince Albert (Bertie)**

The Duke was on time too. He greeted the royal family with a creaky bow. 'Must confess, Ma'am,' he admitted with a grin, 'I'm beginning to change my mind about this place. Not as flimsy as I thought.' The queen wanted to say, 'I told you so,' but managed not to.

The royal party wandered through the long galleries, watching the hundreds of men working to get the Exhibition ready on time. The noise of the bolting, hammering, sawing, and painting was deafening.

The children were amazed by the displays of goods and machinery. Vicky liked the gleaming steam engines best. Bertie was more interested in the men working high up on the roof. Suddenly something caught his eye. 'Look Mama!' he cried. 'Sparrows! There are sparrows inside the Crystal Palace!'

As the queen looked up, she heard a gentle plop! beside her. A browny-white splodge had landed on Bertie's shoulder. 'Ugh!' the boy groaned. 'Look what that stupid sparrow has done on my new coat, Mama. It's ruined!'

The queen turned to the man who was showing them round. 'The sparrows must go!' she commanded. 'Their mess will ruin the displays.'

The man looked worried. 'I know, Ma'am,' he stammered. 'But we don't know how to do it. We can't shoot the birds, Ma'am, because of the glass.'

Victoria looked at the Duke. 'My Lord, you are an intelligent man. How do we get rid of sparrows?' She pointed at the stain on Bertie's coat.

Duke of Wellington

Queen Victoria

'Look Mama!' he cried. 'Sparrows! There are sparrows inside the Crystal Palace!'

'Sparrows?' replied the Duke. 'Simple. Try sparrowhawks, Ma'am.'

That afternoon a hunter brought a pair of sparrowhawks to the Crystal Palace and set them to work catching the sparrows. Three days later not one small bird remained to spoil Albert's Great Exhibition.

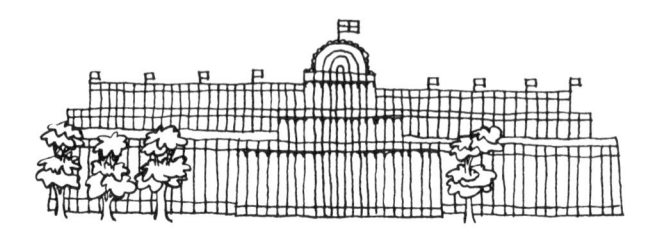

CHAPTER EIGHT

'GOD BLESS QUEEN VICTORIA!'

Queen Victoria opened the Great Exhibition on 1 May 1851. That morning she woke up feeling more excited than at any time since her wedding. Keen to look as magnificent as possible, over her pink and silver dress she wore the broad sash of the Order of the Garter and the Koh-i-Noor diamond – one of the biggest and brightest the world had ever seen. On her head she placed a small crown and two wavy feathers.

Queen Victoria

The showers of the previous day cleared overnight and the sun shone brightly as the queen and her husband drove to Hyde Park in an open carriage. Dense crowds lined the route. As the long procession drove slowly by, the Londoners threw their hats in the air and cheered. 'Long live the

Prince Albert

queen!' they shouted. 'God bless Queen Victoria!'

Thanks to Albert's careful preparations, everything in the Crystal Palace was ready. The glass gleamed in the sunlight. Coloured banners hung from the galleries, fountains played, organs burst into thunderous music as the queen passed by. 25,000 people packed into the building, and more than twenty times that number thronged the streets outside.

As Victoria stood ready to declare the Great Exhibition open, she caught sight of the Duke of Wellington standing unsteadily in the procession. She asked one of her page boys to take him her greetings and thank him again for dealing with the sparrows. The lad did as he was asked and soon came hurrying back.

'The Duke thanks you for your kind thoughts, Ma'am,' he reported.

'Is that all he said?' asked Victoria, who had watched the page talking with the Duke.

'Well, Ma'am,' said the page, looking a bit puzzled, 'His Lordship did say something else. But I don't think I heard it right, Ma'am.'

'What was it?'

'I think he said something about being fond of greenhouses, Ma'am.'

Victoria smiled and bent her head very slightly in the direction of the Duke. In return, he took off his hat and bowed back at her.

~

When their duties were over, Victoria and Albert returned to their carriage for the drive back

'God bless Queen Victoria!'

to Buckingham Palace. Once again the streets echoed to shouts of 'God bless Queen Victoria!'

As they neared the Palace, the queen stopped waving and turned to her husband. 'Dear Albert,' she said in a shaking voice, 'thank you for this wonderful, wonderful day.'

The Prince leaned over and gave her hand a squeeze. 'Don't thank me, Victoria. I have only done my duty. Enjoy this special moment. You hear what your people are saying? They are asking God to bless you.'

Victoria shook her head. 'God bless me? No, my dearest Albert. If anyone deserves to be blessed, it is you. The Great Exhibition is your work, and this is your day. You have made me the luckiest queen and the happiest wife in the world.'

The History File

What happened next?

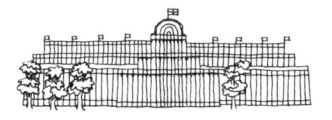

THE GREAT EXHIBITION

The Great Exhibition was a huge success. 6.2 million people from all over the world came to marvel at its galleries of fascinating exhibits. Later, other countries copied Albert's idea and held international exhibitions of their own. When the Great Exhibition was over, the Crystal Palace was taken down and moved to a new site in south London. Here it remained until 1936, when it burned down. The place where it once stood is still known as Crystal Palace, and has given its name to a famous football team.

VICTORIA AND ALBERT

Victoria and Albert had two more children, Leopold and Beatrice. Then disaster. Albert had never been very strong and his health was undermined by years of hard work. In 1861, aged only 42, he died of typhoid fever. Victoria was heartbroken. She retired from public life and for years people saw little of her. Her behaviour attracted a lot of criticism. For about ten years a number of people called for Britain to do away with the monarchy and become a republic, like France.

EMPRESS OF INDIA

Finally, in the late 1870s, Victoria pulled herself together and began to perform her duties again. She was greatly helped by Benjamin Disraeli, the Conservative prime minister. He got parliament to give the queen the title Empress of India. For the rest of her reign Victoria was the much respected head of a huge empire, with relatives in important positions all over Europe. The celebrations to mark fifty years of her reign – the Diamond Jubilee, 1897 – were marked by sincere love for the woman who gave her name to the time when she lived: the Victorian Age.

How do we know?

WRITTEN SOURCES

So many words were written by and about Queen Victoria, it is difficult to know where to begin. We can read the queen's many thousands of letters, as well as letters by Prince Albert, Lord Melbourne, the Duke of Wellington, Sir Robert Peel and other people in this story. There are also all kinds of reports from that time, such as newspaper articles, and records of what was said in parliament and at government meetings.

Then there are dozens of books by historians about Victoria and her times. Many are for grown-ups, but in your school and local library you will also find plenty written especially for children. Most of them have really good pictures, too.

VICTORIAN REMAINS

The first photographs date from Victoria's reign. Pictures taken of the queen show her as an older woman, often looking a bit stern and grumpy. Albert looks quite handsome in his photographs. We have to rely on paintings and drawings to see what the royal couple looked like in their younger days.

Because Victoria died only 100 years ago, there are masses of things left from her reign. The most obvious are the buildings. Windsor Castle and Buckingham Palace, for example, have not changed much outside since she lived there. And the royal family still spend their summer holidays at the castle Albert built at Balmoral. Post boxes marked with the letters 'VR' (there are lots) also date from the reign of Queen Victoria. London has the famous Victoria and Albert Museum, and even Victoria railway station. Most towns and cities have streets named after Victoria and Albert.

Albert is remembered by the Albert Memorial and the magnificent Albert Hall, both in Kensington, south London. The Hall is used for concerts almost every day. As the Prince (and Victoria) loved music, the Hall is perhaps the most suitable way of remembering a remarkable man.

New Words

Baron Important lord
Closet Small room
Courtier Someone who serves the king or queen at court
Cupid The Roman god of love
Duke of Wellington British general who defeated Napoleon at the Battle of Waterloo (1815) and served as prime minister from 1828 to 1830
Gallery Long room
Governess Woman who helps a mother bring up her children of school age
Hanover Small country that is now part of Germany
Hyde Park Large park in the West End of London
Lord Melbourne British prime minister in 1834 and from 1835 to 1841
Minister Member of the government
Napoleon Emperor of France from 1804 to 1815
Order of the Garter Highest award that a British person can be given
Queen Elizabeth Elizabeth I, Queen of England 1558-1601. She never married
Saxe-Coburg Small country that is now part of Germany
Sir Robert Peel British prime minister, 1834 to 1835 and 1841 to 1846
Sparrowhawk Bird of prey that can be trained to catch smaller birds, such as sparrows
Tsar Ruler of Russia, like a king
Wreath Circle of flowers or greenery

TIME LINE

1713 Hanoverians come to the British throne
1819 Victoria and Albert born
1820 Edward Duke of Kent, Victoria's father, dies
1830 William IV becomes king
1837 William IV dies
Victoria becomes queen
1840 Victoria and Albert marry
1841 Princess Victoria ('Vicky') born
1842 Prince Albert Edward ('Bertie') born
1851 Great Exhibition
1861 Victoria Duchess of Kent, Victoria's mother, dies
Albert dies
1877 Victoria becomes Empress of India
1887 Victoria's Golden Jubilee
1897 Victoria's Diamond Jubilee
1901 Victoria dies
Edward VII ('Bertie') becomes king

C.B.E.C.

JERVOIS PRIMARY
SCHOOL